To my husband, Ch[...]
Thank you for all your support. I could n[...]

PRISCILLA & the PERFECT STORM

BOYS TOWN. Press

Boys Town, Nebraska

Written by
Stephie McCumbee
Illustrated by
Kelsey De Weerd

Priscilla & the Perfect Storm
Text and Illustrations Copyright © 2014 by Father Flanagan's Boys' Home
ISBN 978-1-934490-60-0

Published by the Boys Town Press
14100 Crawford St.
Boys Town, NE 68010

For a Boys Town Press catalog, call **1-800-282-6657**
or visit our website: **BoysTownPress.org**

Publisher's Cataloging-in-Publication Data

McCumbee, Stephie.

Priscilla & the Perfect Storm / written by Stephie McCumbee ; illustrated by Kelsey De Weerd.
-- Boys Town, NE : Boys Town Press, c2014.

p. ; cm.
ISBN: 978-1-934490-60-0

Audience: Grades K-6.
Summary: Priscilla is a perfectionist. But when she doesn't achieve perfection, her emotions
get the best of her. With help from her mom, she discovers that success doesn't always mean
being the best.-- Publisher.

1. Perfectionism (Personality trait)--Juvenile fiction. 2. Emotions in children--Juvenile fiction.
3. Success--Psychological aspects--Juvenile fiction. 4. Children--Life skills guides--Juvenile
fiction. 5. [Perfectionism (Personality trait)--Fiction. 6. Emotions--Fiction. 7. Conduct of life-
-Fiction. 8. Success--Fiction.] I. De Weerd, Kelsey. II. Title.

PZ7.M4784153 P75 2014

[Fic]--dc23   1408

Printed in the United States
10 9 8 7 6 5 4 3 2 1

Boys Town Press is the publishing division of Boys Town,
a national organization serving children and families.

Have you ever heard of a "Perfectionist"?

PRISCILLA
the Perfectionist.

I guess that's me.

My mom and dad say a perfectionist sees
every little mistake as a **BIG DEAL**.
And this pretty much sums up –
no, this *exactly* sums up – how I feel.

Everyone says I am very **SMART.**
I knew how to read when I was three!
In school, I even go to a special class
that's made just for kids like me.

All the kids in my special class agree that it's lots of fun,
but sometimes I put extra pressure on myself to always be
NUMBER ONE.

When this happens,
I look around and things
start to change form.

Suddenly everyone is
standing in the *mist* of

PRISCILLA'S STORM

This morning my teacher said,
"Today everyone will draw a picture for his or her dad."
"Oh boy!" I thought to myself.
I knew this would turn out bad.

Everyone says I'm good at art, but
I'm never happy with what I create.
They all say it looks wonderful,
but all I can see are MiSTaKEs!

Eventually, I get really frustrated and today sure was the same. I balled up my painting, tossed it down, and **SCREAMED** my teacher's name.

I could feel my chest tightening.
And then it began...

The room went dark.
I heard the **THUNDER ROAR.**
I could only feel the stress!
And then it **BEGAN TO POUR.**

8

My friends all got upset.
They're so tired of my mess.
Everyone grabbed an umbrella.
Why can't I do my best?

I looked around the room and saw that
everyone was under a desk.
All their papers were ruined.
My storm had caused such a mess!

I grabbed some paper towels and tried to help clean up.
"Just leave us alone, Priscilla," they said.
"We've really had enough!"

In math class that afternoon,
my teacher passed back our chapter test.
"You all did very well," she said.
Then, she laid mine on my desk.

I slowly turned it over. It was even worse than I thought!

"An 88?!" I shouted.

I could feel my face get HOT.

The room went dark.
I heard the **THUNDER ROAR.**
I could only feel the stress!
And then it **BEGAN TO POUR.**

My friends all got upset.
They're so tired of my mess.
Everyone grabbed an umbrella.
Why can't I do my best?

13

The rain finally stopped, and all the storm clouds cleared.
It was too late, though, as everyone's papers were smeared.

My classmates looked so upset with me;
they were soaked through and through.
Of course they're mad – who could blame them?
I'm mad at myself, too.

That evening at the soccer game,
I missed the very first goal.
My team was counting on me,
but my foot slipped – it was
OUT OF MY CONTROL!

"Come on, Priscilla!" I shouted.
"Why can't you get it right?!
Everyone is watching you.

YOU CAN'T
MESS UP TONIGHT!"

Suddenly my throat began to close, and my head started to pound. *And then it began...*

Everything went dark.
I heard the **THUNDER ROAR.**
I could only feel the stress!
And then it **BEGAN TO POUR.**

My friends all got upset.
They're so tired of my mess.
Everyone grabbed an umbrella.
Why can't I do my best?

There was nothing left to do, so they had to cancel the game.

The soccer field was flooded by all the pouring rain.

Everyone was disappointed that no one got to play.

"IT'S ALL MY FAULT," I thought.

"My STORM RUINED everyone's day!"

When I got home, my mom wanted to talk about what had happened.

"I ruined the game for everyone. Didn't you see?" I asked.
"All I saw was someone who made a mistake and then lost her **TEMPER,**" she said.

"You need to work on controlling the storm. It's great that you always want to do things well. But **NO ONE IS PERFECT,** and trying to be will leave you feeling like you have failed."

"I know, Mom, but I feel like I let everyone down," I said.
"Priscilla, I'm not worried about whether you win or lose.
I only care that you tried hard, and that you had fun doing it.
I have a plan to help you deal with your frustration."

"When your chest starts tightening and you feel your heart beating fast, stop and take a time-out.

During your time-out, take three deep breaths and release them slowly. Sometimes, I even count backwards from ten to one in my head.

Try to think about what you did that was positive.

Once you calm down,
it is helpful to talk
with someone about your
feelings. Most importantly,
be willing to try again to be

SUCCESSFUL."

The next day was our school
spelling bee. My whole family was there.
I could feel the pressure building.

I didn't want to let everyone down.
I noticed my chest was getting tight and then
remembered what Mom said last night.

I took three deep breaths to calm myself. Finally, I
walked out on stage. After several rounds, I started

"Priscilla, your word is encyclopedia."

"I-N-C-Y-C-L-O-P-E-D-I-A," I said.
As soon as I finished, I knew I had made a mistake.
"Sorry, that's incorrect," I heard the judge say.

I clinched my fist real tight.
My face started to get RED.

Everyone reached for an umbrella,

JUDGE   JUDGE   JUD

but I remembered what my mom had said!

The room was going dark,
and I heard the **THUNDER ROAR.**
I could still feel so much stress...
But I stopped and said, **"NO MORE!"**

I felt my chest tighten,
and my heart began to pound.
So I took three deep breaths,
   and started
      to count

D
O
W
N.

At first, everything was a blur.
But I focused on what my mom had said.
So I took three more deep breaths
to try and clear my head.

I realized it was working
even better than I thought!
So I quietly walked off stage
to find a quiet spot.

I was sitting alone on the steps,
trying to focus on the things I did right.
When I looked up, suddenly my two
best friends came into sight.

"Priscilla, I can't believe we didn't
have to use our umbrellas today!"
said a smiling Timothy.

"Me, too!" I was proud to say.
"I'm learning to control my storms."

After everyone left, I asked my mom how she knew so much about dealing with frustration. "Priscilla, when I was your age everyone called me 'TORNADO TARA.' I couldn't help that I wanted to be perfect.

But one day my teacher gave me the tips I shared with you. After practicing them all these years, I have learned how to control my temper when I make a mistake. Sometimes I still have a mini-tornado, but the important thing is to allow yourself to fail sometimes."

Mom was right. I guess it takes a lot of practice
to calm the storms.

Thankfully,

I'm a perfectionist.

So I don't mind practicing until I get it right.

Boys Town Press
Featured Titles

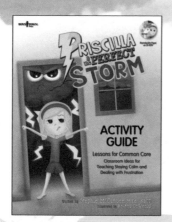

978-1-934490-61-7

978-1-934490-55-6

978-1-934490-54-9

Kid-friendly books to teach social skills

978-1-934490-58-7

978-1-934490-47-1

978-1-934490-62-4

978-1-934490-20-4
978-1-934490-34-1 (Spanish)

978-1-934490-25-9
978-1-934490-53-2 (Spanish)

978-1-934490-57-0

978-1-934490-49-5

BOYS TOWN® Press

BoysTownPress.org

For information on Boys Town, its Education Model®, Common Sense Parenting®, and training programs:
boystowntraining.org
parenting.org
EMAIL: training@BoysTown.org
PHONE: 1-800-545-5771

For parenting and educational books and other resources:
BoysTownPress.org
EMAIL: btpress@BoysTown.org
PHONE: 1-800-282-6657